Chloë's Eggs

By Sue Porter

Look at the pictures. Read the story pointing to the words. Take time to look at the pictures again and talk about them. Here are some specific questions you could ask about this story.

What was the little boy's name?
What was his hen's name?
Why did Robbie's mum get cross with Chloe?
What happened?
How did Robbie feel about his wellies?
Where did Chloe sit in the kitchen?

Can you remember some of the things Chloe did with Robbie's slippers?

What made mum change her mind about having Chloe in the house?

Can you draw Robbie and Chloe?
Can you write their names next to them?

Can you draw the chicks, ducklings and goslings?

Thank you

For my own two
Surprise hatchlings
David and Megan
x x

First published in Great Britain in 1992
by Simon & Schuster Young Books

Copyright © Sue Porter 1992
Designed by Sue Porter

Typeset in 20pt Palatino Roman by Goodfellow & Egan Ltd, Cambridge
Printed and bound in Belgium by Proost International Book Production

Simon & Schuster Young Books
Campus 400
Maylands Avenue
Hemel Hempstead HP2 7EZ

British Library Cataloguing in Publication Data available

ISBN 0-7500-0785-0
ISBN 0-7500-0786-9 pbk

CHLOË'S EGGS

Sue Porter

SIMON & SCHUSTER
YOUNG BOOKS

Chloë, the little brown hen,
laid the loveliest, tastiest eggs.
   Every morning Robbie took them
and placed them carefully in his
little bucket.
   Chloë didn't usually seem to mind.
She just scratched around the farmyard
and then laid some more.

But today was different. She missed
her eggs. She wanted to sit on them
and warm them in her feathers.

She knew that if she did this, fluffy little
chicks would grow inside the shells.
  Chloë sighed and thought how nice
that would be.

But her eggs had gone. She ran here
and there. She clucked and clucked.

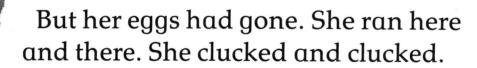

In the ditch lay an old alarm clock
with two smooth, round bells.
   Chloë thought they were her own
smooth, round eggs. She sat down on
them and made a happy, gurgly sound.

"Tick, tick, tick, tick," went the clock.
"DRRRING! DRRRING!" went the bells.
"SQUAWK!" went Chloë.
And she fled indoors.

On the kitchen table lay the shiny,
round iced cakes that Mum had just made.
Chloë thought they were her shiny,
round eggs. She stepped on to the plate
and fluffed her feathers over the sticky icing.

"Shoo!" shouted Mum, too late to save
the cakes.
"Squawk!" grumbled Chloë crossly and
flew outside.

As soon as Mum had gone, Chloë
flew back. The cakes had disappeared,
but on the floor lay Robbie's new slippers.
He thought the round, brown bobbles
were babyish, but Chloë liked them.
They looked like her round brown eggs.
  She sat on them happily.

Robbie came in with his little bucket.
He took out Chloë's eggs and laid them
in Mum's big basket on the table.
In there already were the pale blue eggs
from Louise the duck, and the large,
white eggs from Selina the goose.

"Don't walk about in your wellies,"
Mum said. "Put your slippers on."
 "Do I have to?" Robbie asked.
 But he tugged them out and put them on.
 "Don't blame me," he said to Chloë.
"I don't want to wear them. You can sit
on my wellies instead, if you like."

But Chloë wasn't interested in boots. She wanted her bobble eggs. She followed Robbie wherever he went, watching the slippers all the time. Whenever she could, she tried to sit on them.

She sat on them the whole time that
Robbie ate his lunch.

"Don't pay any attention to Chloë,"
said Mum. "Pay attention to what's
on your plate."

Later, Chloë sat under all the drips
while Robbie washed up.

And while Robbie stood with his feet apart, Chloë flapped back and forth between them. She couldn't make up her mind which one to sit on.

It didn't matter where Robbie put his slippers. Chloë *still* managed to sit on her bobble eggs.

Everyone thought it was very funny.
But Chloë looked rather sad.

"I think she's missing her eggs,"
said Mum. "She wants to sit on something.
She's broody."

"Let's give her eggs back then,"
Robbie said, taking them out of Mum's
basket and popping them under Chloë.

"You should have taken out your
slippers first," said Mum.
"Too late now," Robbie smiled. "I'll just
have to wear my wellies instead."

Chloë stayed in the kitchen and
fussed over her eggs for three weeks.
She was determined not to lose them again.
She was often in the way, but no one tried
to move her.

Until one day, when Robbie heard a tapping sound coming from under Chloë's feathers.

Later, he heard tiny cheeping noises, but Chloë squawked loudly and wouldn't let him look.

Soon, there was so much tapping and so much cheeping that Chloë could not keep her eggs a secret any longer.

"Oh look!" gasped Robbie, as one little
fluffy head after another popped out.
"Ducklings! Goslings! And chicks!"

"You can have your slippers back now,"
said Mum, reaching under Chloë.
  But Chloë had a fierce look in her eyes
and Mum changed her mind. "Er . . . I think
we'll let her keep her bobble eggs," Mum said.
  And Robbie smiled.

And I think Chloë smiled too, don't you?